D1217566

THE HAPPY FUNERAL

RESTAURANT

THE HAPPY FUNERAL

Eve Bunting

Illustrated by Vo-Dinh Mai

Harper & Row, Publishers

The Happy Funeral

Printed in the United States of America. For information address Harper & Row, Publishers, Inc., 10 East 53rd Street, New York, N.Y. 10022. Published simultaneously in Canada by Fitzhenry & Whiteside Limited, Toronto.
First Edition

Library of Congress Cataloging in Publication Data
Bunting, Eve, date
The happy funeral.

Summary: A little Chinese-American girl pays tribute to her grandfather as she assists in the preparations for his funeral.
[1. Grandfathers—Fiction. 2. Funeral rites and ceremonies—Fiction. 3. Death—Fiction. 4. Chinese Americans—Fiction] I. Vo-Dinh Mai, ill. II. Title.
PZ7.B91527Hap 1982 [Fic] 81-47719
ISBN 0-06-020893-7 AACR2
ISBN 0-06-020894-5 (lib. bdg.)

To Christine and Richard with Love

THE HAPPY FUNERAL

Mom says Grandfather is going to have a happy funeral.

My sister, May-May, stares at Mom. "Those words don't fit together. It's like saying a sad party. Or hot snow. It doesn't make sense."

"When someone is very old and has lived a good life, he is happy to go," Mom says.

May-May shrugs. "Just don't expect me to feel happy at Grandfather's funeral," she says.

"Nor me," I say.

"You should say, 'Nor I,' Laura," May-May tells me. She is two years older than I am and loves to show how smart she is.

That night we all go into Chinatown to the funeral home. Inside, there are bunches of flowers everywhere. Some are shaped like hearts. Some like stars.

Grandfather is at the front in his casket. It's open, but I'm not tall enough to see inside. I don't mind. Incense sticks burn in a little row in front of him. They smell good.

REST IN

A lot of people are in the room, and one by one they go up, light a stick, and bow to my grandfather. My Uncle Sydney goes up, and my Aunt Louise. My Uncle Charles and Aunt Janet go with Uncle Albert. All the relatives are here. They give Grandfather a lot of gifts.

I know my grandmother is giving him a map of the spirit world. She puts in some other things too that I can't see. Then she gives him half a comb and holds the other half in her hand.

"What's the comb for?" I whisper to May-May.

May-May pretends not to hear because she doesn't know the answer.

Mom is crying even though this is supposed to be a happy funeral. She has brought food for Grandfather's journey in a little white drawstring bag, which she places beside him. There are soy beans and peanuts and lichee nuts. I saw her fill the bag at the kitchen table.

"Why don't you put in some chocolate chip cookies?" I asked her. "Grandfather loved them."

Mom nodded and put in three. I hope they haven't gone crumbly.

People are burning money, fifty and hundred-dollar bills. The paper ashes fall in the big copper urn. It's just play money, but it will be real when it turns into smoke and rises to the spirit world. Grandfather

will be very rich in his new life. The smoke is hanging around the ceiling. I hope it will get to him.

People are crying. Even my Uncle Sydney is wiping his eyes. Maybe it's the smoke. He burned a cardboard house for Grandfather, a big one with a porch and pillars.

May-May and I have things to burn too. We go up together. She's supposed to help me.

May-May starts because she's older. We spent all afternoon making our pictures. May-May drew a car, a red one with a silver stripe. Grandfather never had a car and she thought he might like one.

"He'll have to learn to drive," I said.

"Spirits don't have to learn anything," May-May told me. "They *know*."

The car picture curls and crumbles when May-May lights it. When it falls, all the ashes puff up and blow around.

I drew Chang. Chang was a dog my grandfather had when he was a boy. He told me about him lots of times. I know Chang was big and black and that's how I drew him. But I printed CHANG on top so there'd be no mistake. I don't want Grandfather to get the wrong dog.

May-May tries to take the stick from me, but I hurry and light my drawing myself. When Chang turns to flame I feel funny, and I begin to cry.

May-May puts her arm around me, and Dad leaves his seat and puts his arm around me too.

When I sit down Mom slips me a Kleenex. I'm ashamed because I'm sort of crying for Chang now, not Grandfather. Being ashamed makes me cry even harder.

But that night in bed, it's Grandfather I'm crying for all right. I'm remembering. The way his hands were dry and shiny. The way he let his side teeth come down to play wolf with me. Grandfather had the kind of teeth he could take out if he wanted to. I think I must have cried in my sleep too, because this morning my hair is wet and Mom has to shampoo it after breakfast.

May-May and Mom and I have black dresses for the funeral. I've never had a black dress before.

We pick Grandmother up at her house. Her dress is black too. She sits beside me and I hold her hand. Sometimes I squeeze it so she'll know I love her.

There are lots of people in the Chinese Gospel Church. Grandfather's here too. Dad says they brought him in the car with the glass sides parked outside. They've brought flowers too, and there's a big photograph of Grandfather framed in roses. He's much younger in the picture. His mouth looks funny. I think it's before he got his wolf teeth.

Mr. Yun, who played Mah-Jongg with Grandfather almost every day, says that Grandfather was an honorable man. Grandfather was great at Mah-Jongg.

Uncle Charles stands up and says that Grandfather was wise and taught him a lot. Grandfather taught me a lot too: how to tie my shoelaces, and how to tell time, and how to let the wind take a kite and lift it to the sky. Grandfather knew how to make kites from old newspapers and dried palm fronds. His best was a bamboo one shaped like an eagle. The kids on Titmus Hill used to shout, "Here comes the kite man," whenever Grandfather appeared.

Uncle Charles is crying when he sits down. Most everyone is. Grandmother's still holding the half comb. Her hand is so small. I never noticed before how small Grandmother is.

"Do you think Grandmother has shrunk?" I whisper to May-May.

"Don't be silly," May-May says.

"Do you think she held the comb all night?"

May-May doesn't answer. Dad leans down. "When Grandmother and Grandfather meet again, the two parts of the comb will be joined," he says softly.

Poor Grandmother! But she can't hold the piece of comb forever, can she? Maybe she'll put it in the glass case with her doll collection until . . . I look up at her and I get

a big lump in my chest. Grandmother is even older than Grandfather.

I can hear music outside, little trills and booms and honks.

The speeches are over. Mom and Dad and Grandmother stand up. Dad takes May-May's hand. Mom takes mine. We walk to the front where Grandfather is. I tell myself I won't look, but I do.

Grandfather's eyes are closed. He's smiling a little. I can see all the gifts set in beside him. One of the things is a rolled-up scarlet kite. I know the kite; when it's open, it has lotus blossoms painted on it and one tiny white bird. Grandmother put it in there for him. He is all covered over with colored cloth squares, like a patchwork quilt. Mom and my aunts made them to keep Grandfather warm. He is not scary at all. He is still Grandfather.

Mother pulls gently on my hand and we go back to our seat. I sit there thinking about his face, and there's something in my mind, something that I saw when I looked at him. I don't know what it is—it's very strange. I need to ask May-May but there's no time. We're standing again, moving toward the door.

A woman gives each of us a candy wrapped in crinkly paper as we leave. "To sweeten your sorrow," she murmurs. Mine looks like cinnamon. May-May's is green.

Dad helps us get through the crowd on the sidewalk. Grandfather's casket is already in the glass-sided car. It's all closed up now. The flowers are in two cars in front and Grandfather's picture is propped on the first car's roof. The band men are in lines of four.

We get into a big black limousine. There are other cars behind us. The band starts playing and the procession moves. And oh, what great music! You'd never guess it was hymns, all jazzed up like this! My feet have a hard time staying still.

Two policemen on motorcycles hold back the traffic so we can pass, then ride along with us.

Mrs. Wing from Wing's Grocery waves and I wave back. Sometimes when we come to the city, we shop at Mrs. Wing's.

The sidewalks are lined with people. Cameras snap. I see that Mr. Wong has two new lanterns in front of his restaurant. They are shaped like fantail fish and he has them lit even though it is daytime. No one is tossing coins into the wishing pool under the red pagoda—they are all too busy watching us. The big stone Buddha outside the Jade Tree Shop is watching us too.

書舘
CHINA BOOKS
WING'S

CHINA BOOKS
WING'S
The FOUR SEASONS

四海兄弟
WON
RESTAU
中山

The band men sway to their own beat. Gold trombones glitter in the bright sun.

It's nice and cool in the big car. This is a happy funeral after all!

But soon we get to the cemetery, and though the band is still playing, I begin to feel bad. There are just headstones now, sliding past our windows. There's a plaster angel with outstretched wings. I move closer to Dad. Tears are running down Mom's face. I want to tell the band to stop playing. Don't they know this place is full of dead people and that my grandfather's dead too?

The flower car stops. The band stops. We stop.

Dad helps Grandmother and Mom and May-May and me from the car.

Mr. Yun and three other men carry Grandfather's casket to a wooden table beside a big square hole. I don't look at the hole. All the flowers are brought out and the picture too.

We stand on one side and the minister reads words. He says Grandfather is going to his spiritual reward. I try to think of the house and the money and Chang. I try to think of Grandfather flying his scarlet kite and how happy he is going to be, but I feel awful.

Now the ceremony's over. There's sniffling and coughing and nose blowing. Uncle Sydney honks loudly into his white handkerchief. Mom hiccups. I look up at her. Then I look at Grandmother. I begin to sob again. May-May's crying too.

I look at Grandfather's casket, blurry through my tears, and I think about him lying inside.

And suddenly I know.

I know what it was I saw when I looked at him. His smile! It's the way he used to smile when I told him one of my Little Gorilla jokes. Or when May-May sat in his lap, which she didn't do too often because she thinks she's too old. Or when we flew our kites, our faces turned up to the sky. He's smiling the way he always smiled when he was happy. *That's* it!

"When someone is very old and has lived a good life, he is happy to go," Mom said.

She never said it was happy for us to have him go.